Stories of Hope and Spirit

Folktales from Eastern Europe

DAN KEDING

August House Publishers, Inc.
LITTLE ROCK

Published 2004 by August House Publishers, Inc.
P.O. Box 3223, Little Rock, Arkansas 72203
www.augusthouse.com

Printed in the United States of America

10 9 8 7 6 5 4 3 2 1 HB

LIBRARY OF CONGRESS
CATALOGING-IN-PUBLICATION DATA

Keding, Dan.
      Stories of hope and spirit : folktales from Eastern Europe /
Dan Keding.
            p.   cm.
      Includes bibliographic references (p.   )
      Contents: The best wish (Croatia)—The most precious gift
(Turkey/Croatia)—The first story (Republic of Georgia)—The
king's ears (Serbia)—Strawberries in winter (Slovakia)—The prince
who married a frog (Croatia)—The three brothers and the pot of
gold (Moldavia)—One man's trouble (Latvia)—The enchanted
princess (Russia)—The old traveler (Estonia)—How a rich man
learned a lesson (Chechnia)—Nail soup (Croatia)—Telling
the stories.
      ISBN 0-87483-727-8 (alk. paper)
      1. Tales—Europe, Eastern. [1. Folklore—Europe, Eastern.]
I. Title.

PZ8.1.K199St   2004
[398.2]—dc 22
                                        2004048700

The paper used in this publication meets the minimum requirements
of the American National Standard for Information Sciences—
Permanence of Paper for Printed Library Materials, ANSI Z39.48.

*To my grandmother, Rose Culap, and all the
immigrants who came to America and
enriched us with the stories they brought.*

*And to Tandy Lacy, my wife and best friend,
who makes every day special.*

ACKNOWLEDGMENTS

I want to thank Steve Kardaleff, my Balkan brother, for his support and friendship; my mother, Ann Keding, for the gift none of us can ever fully understand, the gift of family and heritage; my storytelling friends who have supported and encouraged me all these years—Janice Del Negro, Elizabeth Ellis, Kendall Haven, and Susan Klein; and finally, the folks at August House for truly understanding the importance of these tales.

CONTENTS

INTRODUCTION

Many of the stories in this collection of eastern European folktales came to me through my maternal grandmother, Rose Culap. Noni, as we all called her, came to the United States from Croatia in 1922 and settled in Chicago with my grandfather, Victor. After he died, my grandmother lived with us from the time I was quite young until I was about eleven. Since she had this wild young boy on her hands, she often would tell me stories from the old country that served me well—as lessons, warnings, examples, threats, and just pure entertainment.

Stories filled our house. I would sit in the kitchen while she prepared the dough for her weekly batch of bread and listen to her weave tales of wonder and woe. Down in the basement, where my job was to turn the handle of the old wringer washing machine, I listened to ghost stories. Noni's voice and the *drip, drip* of water made the corners of the basement seem as sinister as Count Dracula's castle.

Noni learned most of her stories from her father and mother, who ran a coffeehouse on the tiny island of Brac off the coast of Yugoslavia. As a child, she served the folks of the village who gathered to drink strong coffee, gossip, and tell stories. Here she often heard stories told by my great-grandfather, the captain of a merchant ship that delivered goods up and down the Danube River. He picked up stories from the men who worked for him and the people he met along the river. It seemed he brought the world into that smoke-filled shop.

Many of the stories included in this anthology come from the Slavs, the peoples of eastern Europe—from the Baltic to the Balkans—who have kept their stories alive in families and coffeehouses, around hearths and campfires, through countless generations of storytellers and listeners who have carried the stories on their lips and in their hearts. I in turn have kept Noni's stories alive in performance, and many of them are in this book. Others I first heard as a boy from elders in our neighborhood or the nuns at school, while still others I have read from a variety of sources. I have tried to list the stories by country of origin, even though most came to me through my family. I hope this prompts you to find other versions to satisfy your curiosity or aid in your own retelling.

These are stories of hope that fuel the human spirit, stories that talk about ultimate victory in the face of great adversity, stories that remind us of the triumph of good over evil in simple or grand ways. All of these stories are part of the experience of eastern Europe, a place that in history has been a battlefield, a crossroads, a place of conflict, and a place of resolution. Each of these stories talks about challenges as well as the strength, wit, hope, and courage it takes to overcome them and succeed. Of course we have our princesses, but we also have our Cinderellas who never marry the prince yet still find happiness. We have kings and princes, but we also have gentle fathers and old travelers who impart great wisdom in unique ways. We have brothers who work together, and we have brothers who are as different as night and day. All these characters revolve around the themes of hope and spirit.

As you read these stories, you may detect a slight variation between these tellings and the well-known versions you have read or heard. My grandmother was a great one for having a lesson in her stories and was often very deliberate in expressing them. When I later heard other versions of these traditional stories, I noticed the differences also. Perhaps in our modern twenty-first-century lives we need a little more of this type of tale. Perhaps we need a little more spirit and hope—and guidance—to open our eyes as we make our way along our journey.

The Best Wish
✡ ✡
✡
CROATIA

Once two angels in heaven were arguing about the souls on earth. One angel, who was a pessimist, felt that all the people on earth were selfish and unworthy of redemption. The other angel, who was an optimist, felt that people were basically good and kind. Finally they argued themselves into a bet. The angel who felt people were selfish bet that the other angel could not find three good, kind people in three days. In that instant, the bet was on.

The optimist disguised himself as a beggar and came down to earth. He began to wander from town to town.

Eventually he came to a tiny village. There he heard of three brothers whose parents had died and left them a meager farm outside of town, a little house to give them shelter, and a beautiful pear tree that was their pride and joy. The fruit from this pear tree fed them and also brought a good price in the market. Each day they took turns, one taking care of the pear tree while the other two worked the farm.

Now the angel, still dressed as a beggar, walked down the road that ran through the tiny village. He came to a small cottage. Its thatched roof seemed to sag under the weight of the sunlight, and its windows were like eyes looking out at the world. The front garden was a sea of flowers surrounding a handsome pear tree. The eldest brother stood on a ladder, pruning the tree and singing to it as he worked.

"Kind sir, could you spare some fruit from your tree for a hungry man?"

The brother looked kindly on him. "This tree belongs not only to me but to my brothers," he said. "But here is the pear I would have had for lunch. You take it."

The angel took the pear. *This is indeed a good and kind man,* he thought to himself. He walked back to the village, holding his pear and smiling to himself.

The next day, the middle brother was watching the tree when the angel approached.

"Kind sir, I am so hungry. Can you spare some fruit from your tree?"

"This tree belongs not only to me but to my brothers also," the middle brother replied. "But you may have the pear I was going to eat for lunch."

The angel thought, *That's two.* And smiling and waving at the second brother, the angel made his way through the village.

On the third day, the youngest brother was watching the tree.

"Kind sir," the beggar said as he approached him, "I am so hungry. Please, can you spare a piece of fruit from your tree?"

"This tree belongs not only to me but to my brothers also," the youngest brother replied. "But you may have the pear I was going to have for my lunch."

The angel was elated. Not only had he found three good people in three days—they came from the same family! As he waved goodbye to the young man, he decided that he must reward the three brothers.

The next morning, the angel appeared at the front door of the cottage, dressed not as a beggar but as a wealthy merchant. The brothers had not yet left for their fields and were amazed at the man now standing at their door. The stranger asked them to take a walk through the countryside with him. He promised that their fields and their pear tree would be well cared for while they were away. The brothers were too awestruck to refuse.

He took the three brothers out to a beautiful meadow, next to a deep and winding river. He turned to the eldest and said, "Make your best wish."

Without hesitation, the young man pointed to the sun-filled meadow and said, "I wish that this was a vineyard, and that I had a winery and many servants who all called me master."

The angel tapped his staff. Vines heavy with grapes filled the valley. A winery rose next to the river, and soon ships filled with his wine were sailing all over the world. As the young man walked toward his new life, the angel called out, "Remember God's poor."

Next, he took the two remaining brothers to an open pasture filled with blackbirds. The angel turned to the middle brother and said, "Make your best wish."

The young man looked over the pasture and said, "I wish that all these birds were sheep, and that I had a mill here and was a wealthy wool merchant with many servants."

The angel tapped his staff. Everything the middle brother had wished for appeared—the sheep and the mill and his servants. Soon ships filled with his wool were traveling all over the world. As the middle brother walked toward his new life, the angel called out, "Remember God's poor."

He took the last brother to the top of a mountain and showed him valleys and oceans and forests. "Make your best wish," he said.

The young man looked around and then looked back at the angel. "I want someone to love me for who I am."

The angel looked at the young man and paused. "That is a rare wish. We'd better look in the book and see what we can do." The angel turned through the pages of his book and finally spoke. "There are only three women in the world who could love you for who you are. Two are married. We'd better hurry to the third."

Soon they arrived at the court of a king whose only daughter was the last of the three women.

"Your Majesty," said the angel, "I have brought a suitor for your daughter."

"Another? I have a king, two princes, and a sultan in the next room. How can I pick the right man?"

Quickly, the angel spoke. "Your Majesty, I have a solution. In your garden you have five olive trees. Cut a branch from each one and plant them in a row. On each branch, tie the name of one suitor. Tomorrow, the branch that is still alive and bearing fruit will also bear the name you seek.

The king thought this to be a good idea. He had the royal gardener plant a branch from each tree. The next day, the king found that four of the branches were dry and withered. But oddly enough, the branch with the young farmer's name was alive and bore fruit.

With much celebration, the young farmer and the princess were married. Afterward, when the angel took them away to a small cottage at the edge of the woods, he told them both: "Remember God's poor."

Time passed, and one year later the angel decided to see how the three brothers were doing. Disguised again as a beggar, he went to the oldest brother's vineyards first.

He knocked on the door. "Please sir, a taste of wine for a thirsty man."

"Away with you!" shouted the brother. "I'll set my dogs on you if you don't leave at once."

The angel tapped his staff, and all of the man's vineyards disappeared. "Go back to your pear tree," the angel said. "You forgot God's poor."

Next, the angel approached the wool merchant's mill. "Please sir, a scrap of cloth to warm my cold shoulders."

"Away with you!" yelled the brother. "Or I'll have my men beat you with sticks."

The angel tapped his staff. The mill and all the sheep disappeared. "Go back to your pear tree. You forgot God's poor."

Finally, the angel walked up the path to the little cottage at the edge of the woods and knocked on the door.

"Do you have a bit of bread for a hungry man?"

Opening the door wide, the young couple took him by the arm and led him to the hearth. "We don't have much, but what we have is yours," said the young woman.

"We have some coarse bread," said the young farmer. But when he brought the bread out of the oven, it was a rich loaf of soft white bread.

"We have some thin soup," said the wife. But when she ladled it out, the soup was thick with vegetables and meat.

"We only have water," they said apologetically. But when they poured a glass for the angel, sweet wine flowed from the pitcher.

The two young people were astonished. Smiling, the angel took them by the hand and led them to the top of a hill. There they looked upon row after row of pear trees and a beautiful house waiting at the end of the row.

"This is for you, and your children, and your children's children, because you remembered God's poor."

The couple embraced. For the rest of their lives, they lived in peace, their doors open to all who knocked. And they never forgot God's poor.

My grandmother would always end this story by reminding me that every wish I made should be my best wish. I would always be careful about what I wished for—at least for a day or two. Even now, I sometimes think of her words and remember to wish for something more than just a new red wagon. So should it be for us all.

The Most Precious Gift

TURKEY/CROATIA

Once there was a sultan who had the most beautiful daughter. She was so beautiful she gave new meaning to the word *exquisite*. He was so proud of her that he decreed that no man could marry his daughter unless he first gave to him the most precious gift in the world. If he was to give up his beautiful daughter, he would have to have something in return.

Kings and princes, nobles and scholars, warriors and travelers came from around the world to the sultan's palace. Each bore what he felt was the most precious gift.

They gave him gold, but he said, "I have chests full of gold."

They gave him silver, but he said, "I have rooms full of silver."

They gave him jewels, but he said, "I have mountains of jewels."

They gave him horses, but he laughed. "I have a stable filled with five hundred horses each with silver bridles and golden saddles."

Soon the suitors stopped coming.

High in the mountains lived an old king who had three sons. One day he woke and called his sons to him.

"My boys, I've had a dream, and in this dream one of you married the sultan's daughter."

"Which one of us?" they cried.

"I don't know," he laughed. "I woke up before it was over. But I'm giving each of you a thousand gold coins to search for the most precious gift."

Now these were not just three brothers; they were also the best of friends. They decided to search for this gift together. They had heard of a magical village high in the mountains and decided to try their luck there. They mounted their horses and rode off.

After a long journey, they found the village. They tied their horses up in the town square and faced the three streets that led from the square.

The oldest spoke. "You take the one on the left," he said to the middle brother. "You take the one on the right," he said to the youngest. "I'll take the middle road. Meet back here in an hour. And good luck to us all."

The three brothers clasped hands and went down their assigned streets. As in most villages, each street was home to a different craftsperson. All the potters worked on one street, all the carpenters on another. The oldest brother went down the middle street, a street where every shop sold only mirrors. The mirrors were beautiful, but he saw nothing precious, nothing truly special.

At the end of the hour, he entered the last shop. As he looked around, he heard a voice.

"Well, what do you want?" There was a small man with a black beard and long black hair. He wore a black robe and a pointed hat.

"Excuse me?"

"I said, what do you want? Don't waste my time, young man."

"Well, I don't think you can help me, but I'm looking for the most precious gift in the world."

"Really? It's in the back. Come on."

"What?" The young man was startled at the answer.

"Never presume, young man. It's in the back."

They went into the back of the shop. The little man rummaged around on a crowded table and finally handed the oldest brother a plain mirror trimmed in copper.

"Here it is—the most precious gift in the world."

"It's a mirror," the brother said. "A plain, ordinary mirror."

"That mirror, young man, is magic. Look into it and think of your father."

The young man did as he was told and soon clouds filled the mirror. When the clouds fell away, he saw his father, seated in his room and reading a book.

"I don't believe it."

"Wonderful, isn't it? All you have to do is look into the mirror and think of someone, and they will appear."

"How much is it?"

"One thousand gold pieces."

The young man handed the little man the money and hurried off to meet his brothers.

The second brother went down the street on the left. On this street, the shops sold only carpets. The carpets were beautiful, but the brother saw nothing precious, nothing special. At the end of the hour, he entered the last shop. He was looking around when he heard a voice.

"What do you want?" There stood a small man with a black beard and long black hair, wearing a black robe and a pointed hat.

"Pardon me?"

"I said, what do you want? You're not here to waste my time, are you?"

"No sir, but I'm afraid you can't help me. I'm looking for the most precious gift in the world."

"You too, huh? It's in the back. Come on."

"It's where?"

"I told you once. Don't make me say it again."

The young man followed the little man into the back room. There the strange man went to a corner and picked out a rolled-up carpet. He unrolled it in front of the young man and smiled triumphantly.

"There it is—the most precious gift in the world."

The young man peered down at the carpet. "It's a rug. It's used. Look, it has stains on it."

"That, young man, is a magic carpet. Sit on it, close your eyes, and think of your father's house."

The young man did as he was told, and when he opened his eyes, he was in his father's room.

"What are you doing here?" cried his father.

"I was in this shop with this little man when—"

The minute he said "little man" he was back in the shop.

"It's incredible."

"It is, really. When you want to go somewhere, you just think of it and you'll be there in a flash."

"How much is it?"

"One thousand gold pieces."

The young man paid him and left to meet his brothers.

The youngest brother went down the street on the right. This was the street where fruits and vegetables were sold. He saw colorful, ripe broccoli and avocados, but none of them were precious. After an hour, he came to the last stand, and as he looked around, he heard a voice.

"Well, what do you want?"

The young man turned and smiled at the strange little man in black.

"Good day, sir, and how are you?"

"I'm fine today. Thank you." The little man was startled at the young man's courtesy.

"I was wondering if you could help me. I'm looking for the most precious gift in the world."

"Of course. It's in the back. Follow me."

"Wonderful," said the youngest brother.

The little man was a bit taken aback at this brother. He went to a table and came back with an enormous lemon.

"Here it is—the most precious gift in the world."

The young man held it gently. "Thank you, sir, for all your help. How much is it?"

"One thousand gold pieces. But don't you want to know what it does?"

The young man laughed. "Of course. How stupid of me."

"This is a magic lemon. Its juice will cure any illness. But use it wisely, for it can only be used once."

The young man thanked him and went to meet his brothers.

They all arrived in the village square at the same time. You may not think that odd, but I do.

"Well, I hope you all got me a wedding present," said the oldest brother, "because I think I have the most precious gift in the world— a magic mirror."

"I have a magic carpet," said the middle brother. "So it could be me."

"I have a lemon," said the youngest.

"A what?" cried the two older brothers.

"It's a magic lemon that can cure any illness. But it only works once."

"Did you try it?"

"Of course not. It only works once. I took it on faith. Besides, I'm not sick."

The other two brothers looked at him and smiled. They loved their younger brother, but he was, after all, the youngest.

"Well, I'm going to see what she looks like." The oldest brother thought of the princess, and when he looked in the mirror he saw she was in bed, surrounded by doctors, her father weeping at her side.

"She's ill, maybe dying."

The middle brother unrolled his magic carpet. "Everyone on the carpet," he said. "And don't forget the lemon."

They were in her room in an instant.

The sultan drew his sword. "What are you doing in my daughter's room?"

"My brothers and I are here to help. With my magic mirror we saw she was ill. With my brother's magic carpet we arrived in a thought, and—I hope this works—our youngest brother's magic lemon will cure her."

The doctors took the lemon, sliced it, and squeezed out the juice. As the princess drank it, the fever disappeared and she was well. But now the sultan had a problem. Who would get her hand in marriage? The mirror showed them she was ill. The carpet brought them there before she could die. The lemon cured her fever, but it was gone now.

It was the princess who solved the dilemma. "Father, the mirror and carpet are indeed wondrous gifts, but the most precious gift of all is life. That's what the youngest brother gave me."

So they were married and lived long and just lives. And the two older brothers took their mirror and their carpet and had a lifetime of adventures.

After she told this story, Noni would always ask me to name the most precious gift. Each time she asked I offered a different answer until I finally gave up and asked her for the solution. She smiled and said, "The friendship between the three brothers. That was the most precious gift. Because of their friendship, they could work together." This story is found in the Balkans but is of Turkish origin. It is hard to separate the Balkans from their Turkish influence, and so I add this story both because I learned it from my grandmother and to honor the Turks whose ghosts still haunt the tales of the Balkans.

The First Story

✡ ✡
✡

REPUBLIC OF GEORGIA

Once there was, once there was, once there was not.

Once, a long time ago, there was a village and in this village there were elders who kept the old stories alive. These were the stories of bygone days, acts of great courage and great love, the old myths that told these people who they were, who they had been, and who they would be.

In this village, there was a boy. This boy loved the old stories, and he loved the old storytellers. Each night, they would gather at one of the elders' cottages, and they would tell stories by the light of the great hearths. They would tell, and he would listen, until the fires died down and the dying embers closed their red eyes in sleep and pulled a black blanket of soot over themselves.

The boy grew with these stories, and unknown to him, they grew in him.

One evening, when the years had passed, the young man sat listening. His eyes were closed, but his vision was with the story. Suddenly the story flew from his mind as the old man who was telling the story stopped and called his name.

"You listen each night to our stories, and the stories have watched you grow as we have. It's your turn, after all these years, to tell us a story, one of the ones you have heard so often."

The young man was shocked. "I can't tell a story," he stammered. "I only listen. I wouldn't know where to begin."

"That part is easy," said the old man. "Each story starts the same way: *Once there was, once there was, once there was not.* Which means that what is true once and twice may not be true a third time. Or maybe it means that what is true for two people is seldom true for the third. Begin."

The young man tried. "Once there was, once there was, once there was not. . . . I can't tell a story. I can't even read."

"Neither can I," said the old man. "People who read lock their stories in books. We keep them alive in our hearts. Start again."

"But what if I forget the words?"

"A story is like a letter. It comes from the past, and we read it and add our words to it and send it to the future. Start again."

The young man tried to start his story. But as he looked around the room and saw those faces he loved so well, creased in wisdom and beauty, his words turned to stones in his mouth. He lowered his eyes to the floor.

The smile on the old man's face faded, as did all the smiles in the room. The elders looked at the young man with sadness in their eyes.

"People who listen to stories but do not tell them are like people who reap the harvest but never sow a seed. They are like people who pick the fruit but never prune the tree. They are like people who wish but never act. Tell us a story or leave."

When the young man heard these words he started his first story, and the smiles returned.

I often tell this story as a link—using it to lead into another story as if the young man begins it himself. It is a wonderful tale about storytelling, and one that I use to illustrate the relationship between the story and the teller and the audience.

The King's Ears

✿ ✿
✿ ✿

SERBIA

Once, a long time ago, but not so long that we can't remember, there was a king. Now the queen was going to have a baby, and the king was worried. He paced back and forth in the hallway of his palace wondering about the child. Would it be a boy to follow him as king? Would it be a girl to follow as queen? Would it be strong? Would it be handsome or pretty? Would the people love and respect it? Back and forth he paced. Finally, the door to the queen's chamber opened and there stood the midwife.

"Your Majesty, you have a son, but . . ."

The king ran past her and never heard what she had to say. He ran up to the bed and found his queen holding out the newborn for the king to see.

"My Lord, your son. He is wonderful, but . . ."

The king never heard her. He looked down at the beautiful baby boy in his arms and shouted for joy. Then he pulled back the blanket to get a better look. He couldn't believe his eyes.

The midwife spoke. "It sometimes happens, Your Majesty. I'm sure he'll grow out of them."

Them were two huge ears just like a donkey's. The king looked at them suspiciously. How could this be? What could he do? The people would never respect, much less obey, a king who had the ears of a donkey. They would laugh at him at every turn. Something had to be done.

The king decided that the secret must stay with the three of them. The midwife, promising never to tell a soul, was given her weight in gold and sent far away to a foreign land where she kept her secret. The little prince was never seen by anyone unless his head was covered. By the time he was six, he always wore a crown that covered his ears. As he grew, the crowns were adjusted. His mother always bathed him and cut his hair. The little prince grew to be a strong, handsome young man . . . and the ears grew with him.

The years passed on. His parents died, and the prince became king. Now his secret was his, and his alone. There was one problem—the royal hair. It continued to grow, but there was no one to cut it. One day he called the royal barber into his chambers. When they were alone, the king took off his crown. The royal barber was shocked. He dutifully cut the young king's hair. When the hair was cut and the crown firmly in place, the king asked the barber if he had noticed anything unusual.

The barber hemmed and hawed. "Well, Your Majesty," he finally said, "you do have ears like a donkey."

Quick as thought, the king's sword leapt from its scabbard and the barber's head rolled across the floor. *Thump, thump, thump.*

Every two weeks another barber was summoned to the palace, and every two weeks another barber disappeared. Finally, after several years, there was only one old barber left in the whole kingdom. On the day he was told to come to the palace, he became very, very ill. He turned to his young apprentice, a boy barely thirteen, and said, "You take my place. I'm much too ill to see the king."

The young boy packed up his combs and scissors, his razor and brushes, and headed for the palace. When he arrived, the guards greeted him with very sympathetic looks.

The king was taken aback that this boy would cut his hair.

"My master is ill, Your Majesty. But I am very good."

Slowly the king took off his crown. The boy thought the ears were wonderful. They reminded him of the stories he had heard of the ancient warriors whose ears grew with each feat and act of bravery. He cut the king's hair, and when he was finished, the king asked, "Did you notice anything unusual about me?"

The boy smiled. "Nothing, Your Majesty."

The king smiled back. "Keep my secret, and you keep your head."

The young boy became the royal barber and the king his only customer. The king liked the boy and confided in him, even asking his advice about dealing with his people. The boy tried to answer truthfully and was flattered that the king trusted him.

But did you ever have a secret so precious that you couldn't tell another living person? Soon the young barber was pale, then sickly, and then he took to his bed, burdened with his secret.

His master, the old barber, came to see him.

"My son, what is the problem?"

"I have a secret that I can't tell a soul."

"You can always tell me."

"If I tell you, we'll both lose our heads."

"Don't tell me!" shouted the old man. "Perhaps you could go to the priest?"

"No. I can't tell anyone."

"You know, when I was a boy, my grandmother told me that when I had a deep, dark secret I could always dig a hole in the ground and tell the earth. It always worked for me."

The boy had nothing to lose. He got a shovel and, leaning on it as though it were a cane, made his way into the woods outside the city. There he found a spot and dug a hole. He knelt down next to the hole and whispered:

The king has the ears of a donkey.

When he stood up, he felt much better. He covered the hole and walked home. But from that hole a willow tree grew overnight, and the next day some children passing by cut down some of the willow's branches to make whistles. The children sold the whistles all over the city, but these whistles didn't play a tune. Instead, they sang a song, and it sounded like this:

The king has the ears of a donkey.
The king has the ears of a donkey.
The king, the king, the king, the king, the king
has the ears of a donkey.

The king was eating his breakfast on his balcony when he heard the song out in the street.

He called his guards. "Bring the young barber to me."

When the barber was brought in and he and the king were alone, the king drew out his sword. "How could you betray me?" he said. "I trusted you."

The young boy pled with the king, telling him exactly what he had done. The king told him to take him to the place where he had buried the secret.

The boy took the king to the spot, but when he saw the willow tree, he was confused. "This wasn't here when I dug my hole."

The king took his sword and—*swoosh*—cut off a branch. He whittled a little flute, and when he blew into it, it sang:

The king has the ears of a donkey.
The king has the ears of a donkey.
The king, the king, the king, the king, the king
has the ears of a donkey.

The king stood there, and he thought. He thought with his heart. He had been a fool. It was time to live the truth. He took off his crown and arm-in-arm with his young barber, walked back to the city so all could see him.

Some people smiled, and others even laughed a little when they first saw him, but he was still their king, and—except for the widows of a few barbers—they all still loved and respected him.

Many years later, when the king passed on, a new king took his place: a king who had once been a barber and had learned at an early age that what a man looked like on the outside was of no importance at all. It was what he had inside that counted.

After my grandmother would tell me this story, we would sing the song about the king's ears as we worked around the house or put the laundry up to dry. Though the Serbian version would have always featured a tsar, she always told it with a king. I learned at an early age that beauty is deep within each of us and seldom is there at first glance.

Strawberries in Winter

SLOVAKIA

Once, a long time ago, a girl named Mareshka lived with her step-mother and her half-sister, Lucy. Life had been pleasant when Mareshka's father was alive. She had beautiful clothes, her own room, and she and Lucy shared all the tasks around the house. Since his death, her step-mother had given all Mareshka's beautiful things to Lucy. Mareshka now lived in a small room behind the kitchen, and all the work about the house and farm fell on her shoulders. She washed and cooked and tended the animals—it was all done by Mareshka.

Lucy, on the other hand, sat in her room day after day looking in a mirror and thinking on her beauty. The shame of it was that Lucy was not nearly as beautiful as Mareshka. All Mareshka's patience and kind-ness, all the goodness and love inside, came out in her face and radiated beauty. Lucy was mean-spirited and petty, and it all showed in her face. All the young men who came to court Lucy were so taken by Mareshka that they forgot about Lucy altogether.

The mother and daughter realized that if Lucy was to ever marry, Mareshka would have to be taken care of.

It was a bitterly cold January night when Lucy came downstairs to the kitchen where Mareshka was cleaning. "Sister," she said, "Mother has bought me that new blue dress, and I fancy violets in my hair when I wear it. Go. Find me some violets."

"Lucy," said Mareshka, "it's winter out there. There are no violets to be found anywhere."

Her stepmother had been listening from the next room. She grabbed her and twirled her around. "Do as you are told, girl. If your sister wants violets, then you go and find them. If you return without them, I will beat you."

The stepmother opened the door and pushed Mareshka out into the cold winter night. She had no cloak or boots to keep her warm. She walked and walked through the pastures and woods, looking for something she knew she would never find. The wind cut her face, and the icy snow snapped at her legs. Finally, deep in the woods, she saw a fire up on a nearby hill. Being half-frozen, she walked toward it. When she got there, she saw a huge bonfire surrounded by twelve stone chairs almost as high as thrones. In the first three sat three older people, in the next three, three middle-aged people, in the next three, three younger people, and in the last three even younger people, barely out of childhood.

Mareshka realized she was looking at the council of the twelve months of the year. The cold finally overcame her fear. She stepped out into the clearing and bowed to the tallest of the chairs, occupied by an old man of grace and wisdom and beauty—the most powerful of all the months, January. His long white hair streamed over his still-powerful shoulders, and his icy-blue pale eyes looked down at her.

"What do you want, child?"

"Please, may I warm myself at your fire?"

He nodded his consent. As she warmed herself he asked her, "What brings you out on such a cold winter night?"

"My sister wants violets for her hair, and my stepmother has sent me out looking for some."

January laughed, and the hills seemed to laugh with him. "Violets in winter? Snow and ice and cold winter winds are everywhere. There are no violets in winter."

"If I do not bring them back with me, they will beat me."

January's eyes narrowed. He turned to his right and said, "Brother March, come here."

March walked forward, and January handed him the wand that he held. The minute March took hold of the wand the snow and ice disappeared, the warm spring winds came up, and a field of violets spread before them.

"Pick them quickly, child," called March.

She picked an apronful, curtsied, and thanked them. Then she ran home.

When she came to the door, her stepmother began to scream at her. "Didn't I tell you not to return until you . . ." Then she looked down and saw the violets in her apron. "Where did you find these?"

"Up in the hills. There were still a few left."

Lucy took all those violets and made braids and chains for her hair. She gave not even one to Mareshka.

The next afternoon, Lucy came down from her room to the kitchen. "Mareshka," she said, "I fancy some strawberries with my lunch."

"Strawberries in winter? Sister, with snow and ice everywhere there can be no strawberries in winter."

Her stepmother emerged from the pantry, grabbed her, and told her to obey her sister. Again she threw her out the door. Again, her parting words were: "And if you return without them, I will beat you."

Again Mareshka wandered through the fields and woods, her heart heavy with despair. And again, just as she was almost too cold to think, she saw the smoke from the fire on the hill. She approached the stone chairs and again asked if she could warm herself at the bonfire.

While she warmed herself, January looked down and smiled, "What are you looking for today, my child?"

"My sister wants strawberries for her lunch."

"Strawberries in winter? There is snow and ice everywhere, child. There are no strawberries in winter."

"If I do not return with strawberries they will beat me."

There was a grim set to January's jaw. He turned and called, "Sister June, come here."

June approached from her chair across the circle, and January handed her his wand. As she took it, winter fell away, spring came and went, and strawberries appeared everywhere.

June spoke gently. "Hurry, child. Pick as many as you can, but hurry."

Mareshka filled her apron with strawberries. Thanking them all, she curtsied and left.

When she returned home, the strawberries filled the house with their aroma. Lucy and her mother could not believe their eyes. Lucy snatched them and, offering none to Mareshka and only a few to her mother, greedily ate them.

Later that evening as the winter storms began to howl, Lucy said to Mareshka, "You have found me violets, and you have found me strawberries. Now go and find me apples, for I want an apple for my supper."

Mareshka started to protest, but she knew it was futile. As she left, she heard her housemates call out, "Do not return without them, or we will beat you!" This was followed by cruel laughter coming from the house as the door shut.

Mareshka again walked through the fields and woods and again came to the circle of stone chairs and her twelve friends and their comforting fire. Again she asked if she could warm herself by the fire. January didn't smile, he just nodded his great head.

"What do they want this time?" he asked grimly.

"Apples. They want apples."

"Apples in winter," said January. "Brother September, come here."

September came forward and took the wand that January offered.

When he touched it the winter ended, the spring and summer came and went, and early fall stretched across the land. There stood nearby a tree, heavy with apples.

"Hurry, Mareshka, take your apples," said September.

But as Mareshka approached the tree, January spoke. "You may only take two, just two apples."

Mareshka shook the tree, and two apples fell to the ground. She picked them up, put them in her pocket, thanked them all, and curtsied. She ran home as fast as she could.

When she got home, her stepmother and Lucy were surprised to see her and even more surprised at the two apples. They bit into them and found them intoxicating, the most delicious apples they had ever tasted.

"Where are the rest?" they demanded.

"I was only allowed to take two," she said.

"You're just lazy. You didn't want to carry them, that's all." The stepmother hit Mareshka and told her to go to her room. Mareshka retreated in tears.

The two of them devoured their apples and could not believe their taste. Lucy spoke first. "Mother, if she could find two we could find more. No one can say no to us. We can keep some and sell the rest in the market for a handsome price."

The mother agreed. They put on their cloaks and boots and warm mittens and left the house. Walking through the winter night, they followed her footsteps until they came to the bonfire and the twelve stone chairs. They never asked for permission to warm themselves; they just walked right up to the fire and ignored the twelve people who watched them.

January knew who they were. "What do you want now, Lucy?" he asked.

"Nothing that concerns you, old man. What I want I'll find on my own and without any help from the likes of you." She and her mother turned and walked into the woods still searching for the apple tree.

January watched them as they left, his blue eyes growing as cold as ice. He took hold of his wand, squeezing it tighter and tighter and tighter. The winds howled, and the snow came, and ice filled the land.

Now Mareshka waited a long, long time for her sister and stepmother to return, but they never did.

Some people say she married one of the boys from the village and settled down. Others say she became a great farmer in her own right. Whichever ending you choose to believe for Mareshka, I'm sure it is happier than the ending her sister and stepmother met.

This was one of my favorite winter stories as a boy. When I tell this story, I always find myself remembering those cold Chicago winters and all that snow. This Cinderella story is found in several Slavic countries. I especially like the idea of the seasons coming to the rescue.

The Prince Who Married a Frog

CROATIA

A long time ago, there lived a king who was cruel and evil. His advisor was a wicked wizard. Now this king had three sons. The oldest was as cruel as his father. The middle son was worse. But the youngest, named Vinko, didn't have a mean bone in his body. He was so kind that most of the people in the kingdom thought he would make the best king of all. They knew, however, that would never happen.

Vinko watched after all the evil deeds his brothers committed. If the oldest ripped up the royal garden, Vinko planted the flowers back and watered them tenderly. If the middle brother kicked the royal hound, Vinko patted the dog and gave him a bone.

Now the king was having money problems as kings often do. He called his wizard to his side and asked him what could be done to find more money to fund the royal excess.

The wizard thought and finally spoke.

"Your Majesty, we are in a dilemma. You see, the normal ways of gaining money are really closed to us. We can't go to war and conquer your enemies because they've all beaten us in battle. We can't raise taxes because the people already pay one hundred percent in taxes. But I do have an idea. We could marry the princes off to three wealthy families. Then we would have their money."

The king liked this idea. "But," he asked, "how can we be sure that the families will be rich?"

"We will issue a proclamation that you are choosing wives for the boys. We'll go to the square, and you will toss your crown into the air. Wherever it lands, the girl who lives there will be the bride. I will use my magic to make sure each one is wealthy and available."

And so the proclamation was made, and the day came when the king and his wizard and the three princes appeared in the square.

The king threw his crown into the air. It swirled and whirled and twirled until, as if by magic, it fell on the roof of the richest merchant in town. His daughter would marry the eldest.

A guard retrieved the crown, and the king threw it in the air a second time. It swirled and whirled and twirled until it fell, as if by magic, on the roof of the richest banker in town. Not only was he rich, but he had plenty of other people's money too. His daughter would marry the second prince.

The king threw his crown one last time. It swirled and whirled and twirled, but it didn't fall on any house. It flew over the city walls and landed in a lake. The king looked at the wizard and said, "Well done, oh wise one. Get in the boat and row me out there."

They rowed out into the middle of the lake, only to find that the crown had not fallen in the water after all but had landed on a tiny island. When the king picked up the crown he found a frog underneath it.

"Good afternoon, gracious King," the frog said.

The king and the wizard were shocked.

"A talking frog?" said the king. "How can this be?"

The wizard had no answers at all. He merely looked at the frog with his mouth wide open.

"I've heard of your proclamation, King, and I have a lovely daughter."

The king's mind turned to evil immediately. What a great way to get back at his all-too-good son and teach him a lesson!

"Bring her to me."

The frog dove into the lake and came back with a beautiful little frog all covered in red and green.

"Take good care of my baby."

"Oh, I will," said the king. "I'll treat her like my own daughter."

When he got back to the shore, he walked straight to Vinko and held out his hand with the little frog in his palm. "Meet your new wife," he said. His brothers howled with laughter, and so did their intended brides, for they were as ill-tempered as the princes.

The next day, the king held a wedding for the three princes. The first bride wore silk, the second satin, and the little frog wore a tiny white veil.

At the wedding dinner, the first princess sipped her soup daintily, the second princess ate her soup sweetly, and the little frog waited for a fly to buzz by and then—*slurp*—the fly was gone. At every meal the little frog would catch all the bugs that flew by, much to the disgust of her fellow princesses and to the growing delight of Vinko.

One day the two princesses, who were fitting in quite nicely in their evil little way, went to the king and demanded that the frog princess be sent away along with her too-good husband. The king was delighted to have an excuse to get his youngest son out of his sight, and he had to admit that the joke had worn thin, especially at mealtime. So he banished Vinko and his bride to a small hunting cottage at the edge of the woods, far from the palace and the city and the king and the royal family.

But Vinko was happy with his new life, and he hoped that his little frog princess was too. Each day he would go off into the woods and hunt and pick wild berries and yams and come home to the cottage. Each day he was amazed when he returned: the house was neat as a pin, a pot of strong tea stood on the stove, and the clothes were washed and neatly folded. Who could be doing all this work while he was gone? Surely not the frog.

One day he decided to solve the mystery. He called out to the frog that he would be back later, took his bow, and left the cottage. He climbed a tree that looked into the cottage and hid among the branches. He hadn't waited long when the frog hopped into view. She looked out the door and gazed in every direction. Then she hopped into the middle of the room and slowly began to grow. Larger and larger she grew until she was as tall as a woman. Slowly she peeled the frog skin off.

A beautiful young woman now stood in the frog's place. She was dressed in a gown of red and green, the same colors as the frog skin and just as lovely. She waltzed around the room and disappeared into the kitchen singing an old song. Vinko sat in the tree in amazement and knew as he sat there that he was in love with his Frog Princess.

The next day, he again hid in the tree. After she had changed and danced into the next room, Vinko ran into the house, took the frog skin, and threw it into the fireplace.

The young woman ran from the next room. "Oh, my prince!" she shouted. "You have broken the spell put on me so long ago, and now I will be as you see, your princess forever."

They danced and laughed and rejoiced at their good fortune. But good fortune is like a good story: it is hard to keep to one's self. Word spread throughout the kingdom that Prince Vinko's Frog Princess was a lovely lady, as kind and as good as he. The people started to say out loud how grand it would be if they could be the next king and queen. These words eventually reached the ears of the king, and he was not happy.

"We have to get rid of them. They are a threat to my throne."

"Well," said the wizard, "I'm sure we can find a way, but we have to be careful. The people have always loved Vinko, and his new bride makes him all the more popular. We must have a reason. We'll give him three tasks to perform. If he fails you—his father, the king—then he and his Frog Princess will be executed."

"Good. Very good. But what can we come up with that will ensure failure?" asked the king.

"I have a few things in mind that will undoubtedly baffle him," the wizard replied.

The next day, the king summoned Prince Vinko to the palace. The royal guards escorted him into the throne room.

"Vinko," said his royal father, "I have a few tasks I want done, done correctly, and done by you. Fail me, and your life and your bride's are forfeited. The first is that I want you to find a pot filled with food that can feed the whole army and still be full after the meal. Go."

Vinko returned home close to tears and told his wife they were lost. When he explained what had to be done, she smiled. "My mother has a pot just like that at the bottom of the lake. Go ask her."

Vinko walked to the lake and called out, "Mother-in-law, Mother-in-law!"

The frog swam to the surface and called out, "Yes, Son, what do you want?"

"Oh, Mother-in-law, I need a pot that can feed the whole army and still be full after the meal. Can you help us?"

"No problem." She dove to the bottom of the lake and returned with a pot filled with steaming, savory stew. She told him to return the pot when he was done.

That afternoon the whole army assembled. Each man was given a large portion from the pot. Yet when the meal was over, the pot was full. The king and the wizard could not believe their eyes. Vinko returned to his princess, dropping the pot into the lake along the way.

The next day, the king again summoned Vinko to the court and again gave him an impossible task.

"This afternoon I want you to bring me a blanket that can cover the entire army while they sleep. If you do not, you both die."

Again Vinko went home in despair and told his wife what his father had asked of him. "What are we going to do?" he cried.

"My mother has a blanket like that at the bottom of the lake. Go ask her for her help."

Vinko went to the lake and called, "Mother-in-law, Mother-in-law!"

The frog rose to the surface and said, "Yes, Son, what do you want?"

"Mother-in-law, I need a blanket that can cover the entire army while they sleep. Can you help us?"

"No problem." She dove to the bottom of the lake and came up with a blanket. She told him to return it after he was finished.

Vinko went to the barracks. The blanket stretched across all five thousand men, even leaving enough room to cover the regimental dog. The king was baffled, and the wizard was mystified. Where could he be getting these magical things? Vinko returned the blanket to the lake on his way home.

The next day, the king and the wizard came up with a task no one could accomplish. Vinko was summoned to the palace.

"Vinko, I want you to take me and the wizard and your two brothers so high we can see the whole kingdom at one time. If you fail . . ."

Vinko knew what would happen if he failed. He went back to his princess and told her the whole story. "We are doomed," he cried. "No one can help us."

His wife smiled. "Go to my mother. She always has an answer for every problem."

Vinko went to the lake and called out, "Mother-in-law, Mother-in-law!"

From the depths of the lake the frog swam. "Yes, Son, what do you want?"

"Mother-in-law, I have to take my father and brothers and the wizard high enough to see the whole kingdom. If not, we are doomed. Can you help us?"

"No problem." The frog called eight huge geese from the other side of the lake and whispered to them.

"Take my friends here with you," she told Vinko. "They will take care of everything."

The eight geese followed Vinko through the streets while all the citizens watched, fearful for his safety.

When they got to the palace gates, the king, his sons, and the wizard waited.

"Well, can you do what I asked?" cried the king. The wizard and the other princes smirked in satisfaction.

"I think my friends here can take care of it all."

Suddenly two geese leapt up and grabbed the king by the shoulders, two grabbed the wizard, and the others grabbed his brothers. Higher and higher they flew until the whole kingdom was in plain view.

"It's beautiful," cried the king. "Now take me down."

The geese all replied, *"Honk, honk, honk."*

"Take me down right now."

"Honk, honk, honk, honk, honk."

"I am the king! Now take me down."

"Honk, honk, honk, honk, honk, honk, honk."

The geese flew to a desert island and dropped the four of them where they belonged. Neither the king nor his wizard nor the two unpleasant princes were ever seen again.

Vinko became king and the Frog Princess his queen, and they reigned in peace and harmony with justice and kindness. The mother-in-law came to live in the palace pond and did what all mothers-in-law do best: she gave everyone advice.

For weeks my Grandmother Noni kept telling me to be careful and not marry a frog. Finally she told me this story. She used to do that a lot— tell me the punchline or moral of the story weeks before she ever told me the actual tale. I guess she wanted to keep me in suspense.

The Three Brothers and the Pot of Gold

✿ ✿
✿

MOLDAVIA

Once, a long time ago, there lived a farmer who had three sons. Now among farmers, having three sons should have been a blessing. These three, however, had little time for farm work. In fact, they had little use of any work at all. All three were strong, healthy, and despite their laziness, good young men. Their only vice, and such a vice it was on a farm, was that they hated work.

When they were young, they would sit under a tree and watch the leaves turn colors. When they grew older, they would watch the young women walk past their farm but were too lazy to ever go out and meet them. When they became young men, they talked endlessly about nothing, and sometimes, when the mood hit them just right, they might go fishing. But, if they caught too many fish, they might leave most behind for it was too much bother to carry them all home.

The neighbors would shake their heads as they watched them stretch out beneath the trees in the yard.

"Why do you not help your father around the farm?" they called.

"Father enjoys his work, and in his work, he provides for us. Why should we work and deny him that pleasure?" The brothers would laugh and eventually fall asleep.

The father tried his best to get them to work but all in vain. The years went on, and finally the old man wore himself out and lay on his deathbed.

"My sons, the end to my work is near. Soon I will leave you. I fear so much for your future."

For the first time, the three young men were roused out of their apathy. They exchanged worried looks. The oldest knelt by his father's side and spoke. "Father, give us your counsel and your blessing. What are we to do?"

The father looked at his sons and slowly spoke. "My boys, when your mother and I were young, we saved our money very guardedly. We knew that hard times might come again and send the wolf to the door. We tried to put one gold coin every month into a small pot that we buried in the yard. As the years went by and you boys came into our lives, we couldn't put any money away and quickly forgot about the pot of gold. I can't remember where, but somewhere in the yard or perhaps in the field next to the house there is a pot of gold. I hope you find it and that it saves you all." With these words, the old man died.

The three sons wept for their father and in their grief kept his memory alive in their hearts for a long time. But soon they were hungry, and the little food and money that their father had in the house was soon gone.

"Our father spoke of a pot of gold," said the middle brother. "I say we start to dig around the house and try to find this gold and keep ourselves alive." The other two agreed.

For the first time in their lives, the three brothers began to work. They shoveled and dug and dug some more. At the end of the first day, their hands were blistered and their backs ached and the places where their muscles should have been were sore, but they found no gold.

They started anew the next day. All week they dug until the whole yard was turned up and the earth was rich and brown—and still they found no gold. They dug even deeper and found nothing. Next they began to dig in the field next to the house. When they found large rocks and stones, they dug them out and rolled them to the side to build fences with. Soon the field was dug, like the yard, rich and brown—and still they found no pot of gold.

The brothers looked around. Finally the eldest spoke.

"It seems a shame to waste all this work. Let us plant a vineyard here and try our hands at a trade."

And so the three brothers planted a vineyard, and they began to raise a small vegetable garden as well. The grapes grew well, and they prospered.

One day, as they sat on their porch after a hard day's work in the vineyard, they sipped their coffee and looked out over their labors. Their vines were heavy with grapes, and their vegetable garden kept their tables full and left them produce to sell.

The years passed and they married, raised families of their own, and taught their children to love and work the land.

One day, when the three brothers had reached their middle years and gray filled their beards, they sat on the porch that looked over their land.

"You know," said the eldest, "there *was* gold in the land. Our father was a wise man."

"Wise, indeed," replied his brothers.

I first heard this story from one of the "other" grandmothers who would meet weekly with Noni. They would talk about the old country or just gossip over coffee and homemade pastries and cookies. Judging by the way they talked about their husbands, I was always surprised it wasn't the mother who imparted the wisdom to the three brothers.

One Man's Trouble

✿ ✿
✿

LATVIA

Once, a long time ago, there lived a farmer. Though he worked night and day, he could never pull himself out of poverty. It seemed that every time he started to feel as if he was getting the best of a situation, he would always fail in the end. If there was a drought one year, there was a flood the next year. If there was disease among his flocks one year, there were wolves the next year. If prices for his grain fell one year, the king raised his taxes the next year.

One day, the farmer sat on a stump and hung his head in despair. All of a sudden there appeared a strange, grotesque creature dancing and singing and laughing in a circle around the farmer. The hair covering its body was matted, its eyes flashed wildly, and its teeth were black. His smell nearly made the farmer weep.

"Who are you?"

"I, my good man, am your trouble. I just came over to make sure you were as miserable as you could be!"

"You monster. Is it because of you that I can't ever succeed?"

"Oh, yes. I am your bad luck, your misfortune. Without me you would be a lucky man."

Quick as a thought, the poor farmer grabbed his trouble by the throat and tied it up with strong ropes. Then the farmer dug a deep pit and threw his trouble into that deep hole. He covered it up with stones and walked back to his house.

By the next day, his luck started to change. His ewes gave birth to twins, his cows began giving twice as much milk as before, his crops grew faster and taller than ever, and his fruit trees were heavy with fruit. All the merchants wanted to buy his produce, and everyone came to purchase his vegetables and fruits and animals. Within weeks, the man who had been so poor was wealthy.

Now this farmer had a neighbor who had always been successful. This wealthy man had looked down on the poor farmer with scorn and had always ridiculed his work. Now he saw that his neighbor was almost as wealthy as he was—and in so short a time, too. One day he could hold his curiosity back no longer. He went for a visit.

"Neighbor, congratulations on your newfound good fortune. I must say I am surprised at how quickly you were able to turn this farm around and make it thrive. What is your secret?"

"It's simple. I found the root of my misfortune. You see, my trouble came to gloat over my bad luck. I caught it and bound it and buried it in a deep pit covered with heavy stones, there by the edge of my pasture. Without a doubt, that is the reason I have finally succeeded after all these years of work and failure."

The rich farmer couldn't stand for his neighbor to finally triumph in life. That very night, he crept to the pit where his neighbor's trouble was buried. All night he lifted the heavy stones and dug through the earth until he found the poor man's trouble. He untied it and set it free.

"Thank you so much!" cried the trouble. "You sir, are a true friend."

"Now," said the rich man, "you can go back and torment your old master once more."

"No, no, no!" cried the trouble. "That man mistreated me and threw me into that pit. But you, sir, were so kind as to free me. You will make a much better master. I'll stay with you forever."

And so it was, and so it should always be.

This one was a bit scary when I heard it as a boy. Noni would always say that when someone's luck was down, we should try and be there for them rather than ridicule or pity them. If we did make fun of them, she said, their misfortune might think that we would make a better master.

The Enchanted Princess

✿ ✿
✿

RUSSIA

Once there was a soldier who had served his king faithfully and truthfully for twenty long years. When the soldier decided to leave the art of war behind him, the king gave him the horse that the soldier had ridden and the sword that had served him well in many a battle.

The soldier set off for his native home. He traveled a day and he traveled a week, but still he was far from his home. The soldier had neither money nor food and was getting desperate. One day, he saw a mighty castle. Thinking to hire himself out to the lord of that estate until he had saved enough to continue his journey home, he rode into the courtyard—but no one met him. He stabled his horse and fed him.

The soldier walked into the main hall. A feast was set out, waiting for him. The soldier ate his fill and rested before the blazing fire in the fireplace. Just before he dropped off to sleep, he heard a noise. He was startled to see an enormous bear walking upright into the room. The soldier slowly drew his sword, but the bear just seemed to dance around the room, ignoring the soldier. Finally it stopped and turned its sad eyes toward the soldier and spoke.

"Fear me not, brave hero, for I am not what I seem."

The soldier sheathed his sword and slowly sat down, listening quietly to the bear's story.

"There was a time when beauty and grace and peace ruled this land. But evil is always jealous of such places, and a wizard came who enchanted my kingdom. I am a princess, under this spell, as are all my people. If you spend three nights alone in this castle, the spell will be broken and I will be returned to my natural form. I will share my castle and estate with you and call you friend and husband forever."

The soldier was moved by this tale and promised to stay the three nights and break the spell.

Now the first night, there fell upon him such a sadness that the soldier wept and wept and longed for days that never had happened. The second night, there fell on him such a loneliness that he ran from room to room looking for someone, for anyone whom he might talk to, someone to break the horror of being so alone. The third night, the soldier saw monsters in every shadow, in every corner, and ran through every room away from the terror that chased him.

When he awoke after the last night, the princess stood before him, a woman of unspeakable beauty. Her servants prepared him food. The soldier and princess talked and talked all day and into the next. Each had truly found a best friend in the other. The soldier and the princess were married and began to rule the kingdom together.

✿ ✿
✿

One day, the soldier began to yearn for his homeland, to see once more his aged parents and brothers and sisters. The princess tried to dissuade him, but in the end, she let him go. Before he left, she spoke to him about his journey:

"My friend and husband, as you travel on your journey, throw these seeds on either side of the roads you pass. Wherever they fall, trees will spring up in an instant with beautiful fruit hanging from every branch, wonderful birds singing in every bough, and an old tomcat at the trunk, telling tales from far across the sea." She handed him the bag of seeds, and he promised her that he would be back in three months.

The soldier journeyed toward his parents' home. As he rode, he scattered the seeds on either side of his path. Forests rose as he passed and the fruit ripened and the birds sang and stories were told.

✩ ✩
✩

One day, the soldier saw a strange sight. Off to the side of the road, some merchants had stopped and were passing the time of day playing cards. Nearby a pot was boiling though no fire burned beneath it.

Now the soldier thought that this was indeed magical. He couldn't resist boasting of his own enchanted seeds. He rode over to the merchants and dismounted.

"Good day, gentlemen, and what a glorious day it is."

The merchants agreed, and the soldier continued. "I see that you possess a most wondrous cooking pot. I too have a magical bag of seeds that allows me to plant forests wherever I travel. My dear friend and wife gave it to me as a traveling gift."

The soldier produced a seed from the bag and dropped it on the ground—at once a tree sprang up, laden with fruit, inhabited by birds, with a tomcat telling tales beneath it.

Now the merchants were actually sorcerers of the most evil kind, the very men who had put the spell on his wife many years before. When they saw that bag they knew who the soldier's wife was and that this was the very man who had broken the spell. They invited him to join them for tea and then slipped a potion into his cup. The soldier fell asleep, and the wizards took his bag and put it into their own wagon.

"That will teach the meddling fool. He'll sleep for six months and a day."

They left him sleeping under the tree while the birds sang and the tomcat told his tales.

✩ ✩
✩

After three months, the princess began to worry that her friend and husband would not return. She rode out into the world and came to the first forest that he had planted. The tops of all the trees had withered. The songs the birds sang were weak, and the tomcats were silent. She traveled on and found that each forest was the same—dying. At last, she came to the tree he planted just before the wizards put a spell on him. There he lay beneath the tree, sound asleep.

His wife tried to wake him but was unable to. She thought that he was ignoring her. Finally she spoke.

"I have worried about you for so long, and now I find you asleep and not even willing to speak to me. I wish that a great wind would take you far away and teach you a lesson."

No sooner had she spoken than a wind took her husband up into the sky and disappeared with him. As soon as he was out of sight, she was grief-stricken that her anger had gotten the best of her. The little tomcat under the tree told her the story of the evil magicians, and she began to weep. She made her way back to her castle and went into mourning.

Now the soldier was carried by the wind beyond the thrice-ninth land, to the thirtieth kingdom, and left on a strand of land between two seas. If he rolled either way, he would plunge into the waters and be only a memory.

✿ ✿
✿

The good hero slept for six months and a day and moved not a finger. When he woke, he sat straight up and looked on both sides of him. He wondered at first how he came to be there. Then he remembered the strangers and thought to himself that in some way it must have been their doing—and in a way, he was right. He walked along the strand until he came to a mountain shrouded by mist and clouds. When he reached the top, he saw three giants fighting and screaming at each other.

"Hold, neighbors. What has come between you to cause such anger?"

The giants stopped and looked at the soldier. "Our father died three days ago and left three gifts for us, but we cannot divide them. He left a magic carpet that can fly anywhere in the world, a pair of swift boots that can take us running anywhere in a matter of minutes, and a cloak that will make us invisible."

"You are fighting over such little things? Please, let me settle this argument, and trust me that when I am finished, no one will complain."

The giants agreed to his judgment.

"I want you to bring me the biggest cauldron you have. Fill it with pitch and set it to boil."

The giants did as they were told, and soon the pitch was bubbling over the top of the huge pot. The soldier ladled the pitch over a nearby boulder until it was covered.

"Now I am going to roll this stone, covered with pitch, down the mountain. The first one to catch it and bring it back gets the first choice."

The soldier sent the boulder down the mountainside. The minute the giants started running after the stone, the soldier emptied the entire cauldron down the mountain behind them. Soon their feet were covered in pitch. As it hardened, they were stuck fast and couldn't move.

"Thank you, my friends, for the lovely gifts." The soldier sat on the magic carpet with the boots and cloak and sped away, followed by the curses and cries of the giants.

The soldier flew for several days. He knew that he needed the aid of someone with great knowledge to find the kingdom of his friend and wife.

Soon he came to a hut. Instead of a foundation, it sat on one long chicken leg, surrounded by a fence, each picket crowned with a skull that spoke his name when he drew near. He entered the hut, and there sat the witch Baba Yaga.

"Greetings to you, Grandmother. I have traveled and been

deceived by wizards. I am far from my own country and long to be with my wife and friend. With your great wisdom, can you help me return to my princess?"

"There will always be a place at my table for you." Baba Yaga was pleased by his flattery and summoned the winds that flew at her bidding. When they were all swirling around her hut, she walked out and asked them if they knew where the princess might be dwelling. At first, none of them spoke. At last, the South Wind broke the silence.

"I have seen the princess weeping in her palace, surrounded by suitors—by tsars and kings and their sons—all wanting her hand. They drink and eat all day long waiting for an answer, but she weeps for her lost love."

"Is it far?" asked Baba Yaga.

"Fifty years with the magic carpet and twenty years with the swift boots."

The soldier wept at the words the South Wind spoke.

"Great Wind, can you fly me to my home?"

The South Wind roared its answer. "If I do this for you, then you must let me ravage your kingdom for three days."

The soldier agreed, and the South Wind bore him up. They traveled like thought and soon arrived in the woods just beyond his castle.

"Great Wind, you have kept your promise. Now I'll keep mine."

The South Wind was so moved by the soldier's love for his wife and his honor in keeping his promise that it spoke. "I'll not ravage your lands. If I were to blow through these hills and valleys not a tree would stand, not a house would be safe."

The soldier thanked the South Wind. He put on his cloak of invisibility and walked toward the castle.

When he arrived, it was just as the South Wind had told him. Kings and tsars and their sons feasted on his wife's food and drank her wine. She sat at the head table with a tear-stained face. The soldier walked through the crowd unseen. Each time a lord put a glass to his lips, the soldier knocked it from his hands and it flew across the room.

Everyone wondered at this magic. His wife smiled, knowing that her friend and husband was in the room. She stood and looked at the assembly and spoke.

"I have a riddle, and whoever answers it correctly, that man I will marry.

"I had a homemade casket with a golden key; I lost the key and did not find it; now the key has found itself. What is the key, and what is the casket?"

All the kings and tsars and their sons thought and thought, but none knew the answer.

"Show yourself, my friend and husband."

The soldier took off the cloak, walked to his wife's side, and kissed her deeply.

"Here is the answer. I am the homemade casket, and my faithful friend and husband is the key."

All the nobility left, and the princess and the soldier lived out their lives in peace and harmony.

As with many epic tales, I heard bits and pieces of this story, here and there, as a boy. The story is filled with the wild fantasy so common to those great folktales from Russia. Here are princesses and soldiers seeking their fortunes, wicked wizards and giants—and we even have an appearance from a kindly Baba Yaga (hard to believe, since most stories portray her as a wicked witch). The end of this story always reminds me of Odysseus's return to Penelope.

The Old Traveler

✡ ✡
✡

ESTONIA

Once, so long ago but it seems like yesterday—not your yesterday nor mine but someone's—a poor old man traveled along the road. Night was coming on and with it the cold and damp that chills the bones. Now in those days, it was the custom to stop at a house on the road and ask for lodging. So when the old traveler saw a large house, he knocked on the door.

Now the rich woman who lived there looked out and saw this tired, dusty traveler. "Why do knock on my door, old man?" she called out.

"Kind woman, can you give me shelter for the night?"

"Give you shelter? I'll let the dogs loose, that's what I'll do. Now off with you."

Wearily the old man moved on. Soon he came to another house, this one a humble cottage. The old traveler could hear singing and laughter coming from inside. He knew this house was filled not with wealth but with joy. *Perhaps here,* he thought.

He knocked at the door. A boy answered the door.

"Please, could you give me shelter on this cold night?"

"Come in, Grandfather."

The mother welcomed him, surrounded by her smiling children.

"We don't have much room, and the children are in a singing mood, but you are welcome."

The children took his damp coat and hung it near the fire to dry. The children entertained the old man as they sang and carried on. Their clothes were ragged and threadbare. The old man asked the mother about their plight.

"If I could, I would sew them new ones," said the mother. "I was once a well-respected seamstress. My husband died two years ago, and now we can barely feed ourselves, let alone buy cloth to make new clothes."

The mother laid out a small supper, but the old man told her he had already eaten and in fact had some left. He reached into his pack and brought out sausage, bread, and cheese to share with her and her children.

When it was time for bed, he began to unroll his sleeping blanket. The boy who had met him at the door spoke. "No, Grandfather. You sleep in my bed, and I'll sleep here. I could never rest knowing you slept on the floor." And so the old man slept in the boy's bed, and he slept well.

In the morning, the old man had some hot tea and thanked the woman.

She walked him to the gate to bid him farewell.

"I have a gift for you," said the old traveler.

"We weren't being kind in order to get a reward," said the young mother.

"If you had, you wouldn't be getting one. Now listen: that which you do first thing in the morning you will do until evening."

He smiled and waved and continued his journey.

But as soon as she returned to the house, she forgot his words. She decided to try and make at least one shirt from some cloth she had in her chest. She began to pull a piece of cloth from her old box of scraps. But the cloth she pulled was the finest silk she had ever seen. She pulled for hours, and silk of all the colors of the rainbow appeared, then wool of every pattern imaginable, then cotton of every color under the sun. She sent her son to borrow a measuring stick from her rich neighbor. All day long the woman pulled cloth from the box until it filled the house up to her knees.

By the end of the day, she had not only enough cloth to make clothes for her family until the end of their days but enough to make clothes to sell to others. She now understood the old traveler's blessing. They would never be poor again.

When she returned the measuring stick to her neighbor, she told her the story of her good fortune.

The rich woman thought to herself that she had been a fool. Why had she been so hasty in sending the old man away the day before? She deserved to have that kind of luck, not her neighbor. She sent a servant out looking for the old tramp. When he found him, the old man didn't want to return.

"If I come back without you," said the young servant, "my mistress will take my wages from me and my position, too."

The old man took pity on the young man and returned with him.

When they arrived, the rich woman met them at the gate, bowing and smiling. She took the old traveler into her house and fed him a wonderful meal of sausage and cabbage, chicken and dumplings, soup and bread. After dinner, she showed him to his own room with a soft bed and clean sheets. He stayed with her for three days, quietly eating and drinking and smoking his pipe as he watched her run her household. He overheard her harsh words to the servants when she didn't know he was listening. He saw her kick the old lame dog when she didn't know he was watching. Each day, she became more anxious for him to leave and give her a blessing. Finally on the fourth day he set off on the road again.

She couldn't contain herself. "Tell me, Grandfather. What is my gift?"

He turned. With a smile that was both sad and sly, he told her, "That which you do this morning you will do until evening." With that, he walked down the road.

The rich woman was so happy. She rushed into her house and ran up the stairs to the attic where she kept her money chest hidden. She would count her money all day and be so much richer by nightfall. She pulled the chest from its hiding place in the rafters. As she did so, dust flew from the rafters in every direction. She lowered the chest to the floor, but before she could even open it, dust flew up her nose and she sneezed.

And she sneezed again. And again. And again. Every time she sneezed, the dust rose and she sneezed again, each time louder than the time before.

She sneezed, and the chickens refused to lay eggs.

She sneezed, and the cows stopped giving milk.

She sneezed, and the horses ran away.

She sneezed, and the dogs hid in the woods.

She sneezed, and the servants covered their ears and ran off to their homes.

She sneezed, and the windows shattered, and the walls of her house began to crumble.

And so she sneezed until nightfall. And when she finally sneezed one last time, the rich woman sat alone in the ruins of her once-fine house. The lesson was not lost on her.

This story is found in many cultures. As a child, I heard it often from my grandmother and her friends. The first time I encountered it was in a play I acted in, Why the Lord Came to Sand Mountain. *I played God— a hard act to follow ever since creation.*

How the Rich Man Learned a Lesson
✿ ✿ ✿
CHECHNIA

Once, a long time ago, in a village high in the mountains, a man named Hamid lived with his beautiful wife, Zeinai. Though the couple was very poor, they worked hard and delighted in each other's company and love.

Everyone took delight in their happiness—everyone, that is, but the only rich man in the village, an old miser who took no joy in anyone's happiness. All he could do was complain that such a poor man should have such a beautiful, loving wife.

One day, Hamid went into the forest to gather some firewood. As he walked through the woods, he came upon a clearing, and there he spied two of the most enormous melons he had ever seen. It wasn't just their size that was notable; it was so late in the season that the melons in all the village gardens had already been harvested and eaten.

Hamid picked one of the melons and staggered home to surprise his wife.

"My dear!" he called. "See what I have found in the woods today!" He took a knife and was about to slice the melon when Zeinai called out.

"Hamid! Melons this size are rare—and even moreso this time of year. I think we should sell it and use the money to buy bread and cheese and some seeds for next year."

Hamid agreed with his wife that selling the melon was a wonderful idea. He decided to take it to the old miser, the only man in the village with any money.

The rich man enjoyed food second only to wealth. When he saw the melon, he took out his purse and paid a handsome price for it.

"Have you any more like it?"

"There is another where I found this one," said Hamid.

Now the rich man saw an opening for his own desires.

"Bring it to me, and I will pay you well. In fact, I will give you the first thing you touch in my house. But remember, if you fail to bring it to me I will come to your house and you will give to me the first thing I touch."

Without thinking, Hamid agreed. He returned home to his wife and told her of the arrangement.

"When I bring him that melon, I'll touch his purse, and we will never want again."

"Do you remember where you found the melons?" Zeinai asked.

"Yes, of course. In the woods just to the south of the village, in a small clearing."

"Then go there and hurry, for I don't trust the rich man. If we fail to get that melon he will come here and touch me. I have seen how he looks at me in the market and at church."

As they talked, they never saw the rich man's two servants listening outside their window. When they heard of the location of the other melon, they were off as fast as they could run. They found the melon and brought it back to the miser.

When Hamid came to the field, he found only the empty vine. The other melon was gone. He was heartbroken. He couldn't bear to face his wife. The thought of losing her weighed him down so much that he began to wander through the woods. He came to the river, and as he walked along its banks, he heard a cry for help. Hamid looked up and saw an old man being carried down the river, struggling to keep afloat.

Hamid dove into the water and pulled the old man to safety. Over and over again, the old man thanked him.

"I can never repay your kindness," said the old man, "but I must try."

"No man can help me, Grandfather. I am cursed this day." Hamid told the old man his story, tears streaking his face.

The old man sighed. "It was a foolish bargain, but listen to me. Go home and hide your wife in the attic. Make sure that the ladder to the attic is old and unsteady. Then ask the neighbors to come to your house. When all is in place, invite the old rich man to come to your home. I think he will go home without your wife but with a very old ladder."

Hamid smiled and shook the old man's hand. He ran home and told Zeinai what had happened. She hid in the attic, and Hamid called all the neighbors to his home. When all was ready, he called on the rich man to come and get his prize.

The rich man came quickly, hands tucked into the folds of his long robe. "You remember our agreement?"

"I do," said Hamid. "Whatever you touch first belongs to you."

Keeping his hands deep in his robe, the rich man carefully walked through the house. He stopped when he heard Zeinai singing in the attic.

"Come down and join us," the old miser called.

"I cannot," she replied. "I am afraid of falling down the ladder."

"I'll come up myself and help you, my dear."

The rich man started to climb up the ladder, careful not to touch it with his hands. When he was halfway up, the old rickety ladder began to sway, slowly at first and then more and more violently.

The old miser began to shake with fear himself. Forgetting his agreement, he reached out with both hands to steady himself.

Hamid cried with joy. "You have made your choice. The ladder is yours."

The neighbors agreed in chorus that it was a wise choice.

The old man went home with his new old ladder, and the neighbors had a feast for the happy couple whose love made them all so rich.

This story from Chechnia celebrates both the triumph of the peasant over the wealthy and the wisdom of our elders. The village would have been a lesser place without the love these two young people shared.

Nail Soup

✿ ✿ ✿
CROATIA

Once, a long time ago, there was a war. Two countries came together and fought for twelve long years until both kings ran out of money. When the money was gone, they declared peace and sent their armies home. But they had no way to pay their soldiers. They gave every man his uniform, his musket, his sword, a loaf of bread and a square of cheese and said, "Thank you very much."

Now some soldiers could walk home in a day or two, some in three or four. One soldier, however, lived on the other side of the kingdom. It would take him weeks to walk home. After a few days, his bread and cheese were gone and he was hungry. He came to a small village and said to himself, *I fought for these people for a dozen years. I'm sure they will give me something to eat.*

He knocked on the first door. An old man, wrinkled and bent with age, answered the door with a frown on his face. "What do you want?" he asked.

"I'm a soldier come home from the war. I was wondering if you could help me with a piece of fruit or some bread and cheese? I'm hungry."

"Go away," said the old man. "We hardly have enough to feed ourselves." He slammed the door in the soldier's face.

That's too bad, thought the soldier.

He went to the next cottage and knocked on the door. A young woman answered the door, her frown as awful as the old man's. "What do you want?"

Doesn't anyone know the word "hello"? thought the soldier. "I'm a soldier come home from the war, and I'm hungry. I was wondering if you could spare some food? I'll work for it. I'll cut wood or carry water or—"

"Go away," she interrupted. "I can't spare a thing."

The soldier went to the next door and knocked. A little boy, wearing the same frown, answered the door. "What do you want?" he asked sharply. He had learned his lessons well.

"I'm a soldier come home from the war, and I was wondering if you could help me."

"Go away." The boy slammed the door.

The soldier went to every cottage in the village and got the same answers: *"We don't have enough to share." "Go away." "Leave us alone."* When he looked into their back yards, however, he saw big gardens full of produce, trees heavy with fruit, chickens and goats and cows. They had plenty to spare, they just wouldn't share with him.

He still had his sword and musket. He could have taken anything he wanted, but he wasn't that kind of man. He decided to go to the next town and see if the people there were friendlier. Before he left, he stopped to rest in the park at the center of the village. He took off his tall hat and rested his musket against a bench. Then he unbuckled his sword belt, opened his jacket, and stretched out his long legs.

As he sat, he detected a sweet smell all around him. He looked down and saw that the bench he sat on was brand new, probably made that very day. The sawdust and new wood combined to make a wonderful smell. As he looked down, he saw a pile of carpenter's nails. *This is a find,* he thought. *I've been gone all these years. I'm sure I'll need to make a few repairs around my house. Too bad it's not food, though.* As he slipped the nails into his pocket he got an idea—perhaps, in a way, the nails *were* food.

He jumped up on the bench and started to call out.

"People of the village—come out, come out, come out! I have a gift for you."

The people peeked out their windows and opened their doors just a crack.

"Don't be shy," he called. "It's free!"

When the people heard the word *free,* they all came out—every man, woman, and child.

The soldier smiled down at them all and spoke. "I am a soldier come home from the war. Not too long ago, I went around the world in one day. I had breakfast with the Emperor of China, tea with the Emperor of Japan, and dinner with the Queen of America. All these very important and powerful people share a secret. They all have a bowl of very special soup each day. It makes them happy and wise. I have the recipe. The Queen of America gave it to me, and I'm going to make it for you."

The people cheered. "What kind of soup is it?" they asked.

"Nail soup," he cried.

The people shook their heads in bewilderment. They had never heard of nail soup. Even the best cooks were perplexed.

"You've never heard of nail soup?" asked the soldier. "It's very high in iron. Well, if you don't want me to make it for you I'll go on to the next village and make it there."

The people begged him to stay and make his wonderful soup for them.

"Fine. We'll need a few things. First, a pot big enough to feed the whole village."

"My sister has a cauldron in her back yard."

The men from the village dragged it into the park. Some children ran off with buckets and began to fill the cauldron with spring water.

Others brought wood and started a fire. Soon the water was beginning to bubble and boil.

"Do you put the nails in now?" they asked.

"Not yet. Too bad this is such a poor village and you have nothing to share. There are some ingredients that make nail soup just delicious."

"Like what?" asked the villagers.

"Well, if we had some potatoes and carrots that would be nice."

The old man he first met went and got a big sack of potatoes. The young woman who had turned him away came back with a huge bunch of carrots. The soldier cut them up with his sword and put them into the pot.

"Now you put the nails in?"

"Not yet. You know what makes nail soup really good?"

They shook their heads no.

"Some onions and tomatoes."

People ran to their homes and brought back dozens and dozens of onions and tomatoes. He cut them up and threw them into the pot. The smell was inviting.

"Now you put the nails in?"

"Not yet. You know what makes nail soup really good?"

Again they all shook their heads no.

"Some zucchini and spices."

Everyone had zucchini. They brought back dozens, as well as garlic, salt, pepper, and oregano. The soldier cut up the zucchini and poured in the spices. The smell was captivating.

"Now you put the nails in?"

"Not yet. You know what makes nail soup perfect? If we had some meat. Any leftovers will do."

All the people ran back and came back with beef and chicken, pork and duck. The soldier cut it up and put it into the pot.

"Now, everyone go home and bring back a bowl and a spoon for yourselves, and would one of you bring back an extra one for me? Don't forget to bring something to share—bread, fruit, cheese, wine."

All those people who had been so sour and unfriendly laughed and skipped back to their homes. They came back with bowls and food to share with their neighbors. They stood in line and one by one, the soldier gave each of them a bowl of soup. Some people had two bowls, some three; the soldier had four. They sat in the park and ate their soup and shared their food. People started to sing, some started to tell stories, and one man went home and brought back his fiddle, and soon the folks were dancing.

Suddenly, one little boy yelled at the top of his voice.

"Wait a minute! He didn't put the nails in."

Everyone stopped and stared at the soldier. Slowly he took the nails from his coat pocket and gently put them into the hand of the boy.

"You're right, I didn't. But you keep the nails, son, and next time someone comes to your door hungry, you'll know just what to do."

The people shuffled their feet and looked away.

Then the music started again, and the stories and songs and dances all flooded back, this time to stay.

The soldier was right. Nail soup makes everyone very happy and very wise.

Sometimes when my grandmother would cook soup, I'd ask over and over as she added ingredients, "Is it done yet?" And she would answer, "Not yet." After she added the final ingredient, she would look at me and ask if I thought we should put in the nails. I knew better—her soup was too good to ruin with nails. This variation on the Stone Soup story is found widely in eastern Europe.

TELLING THE STORIES

Passion and drama, wisdom and humor, are all present in these stories. When you tell these tales, trust them to take you and your listeners to that special place where the story finds its voice. Let the story travel through you to your audience: don't push the story or force it; don't feel that the story needs you to be overly dramatic or athletic; don't change the truth of the story to make it "better." Generations and the ages have already done your editing for you. You want your audience to be impressed not with your acting ability but with the story, to take it home with them.

Remember, the tale will be around long after you're gone. What the story needs from you is for you to allow it to pass through you and into the hearts and imaginations of your audience. Be gentle and honest with these tales, and you will become part of an unbroken chain that runs through the history of these proud and beautiful people.

BIBLIOGRAPHY

This selection of books contains more stories from eastern Europe and is a treasure trove for the storyteller and story lover alike. Please note that the spelling of Yugoslav/Jugoslav is correct in either form.

Afans'ev, Aleksandr. *Russian Fairy Tales*. New York: Pantheon Books, 1975.

Biro, Val. *Hungarian Folktales*. Oxford: Oxford University Press, 1992.

Chodsko, Alexander. *Slav Tales*. London: Ballantyne, Hanson & Co., 1896. A very old collection worth the search.

Cooper, David L., ed. *Traditional Slovak Folktales*. Armonk, New York: M.E. Sharpe Co., 2001.

Curcija-Prodanovic, Nada. *Yugoslav Folktales*. Oxford: Oxford University Press, 1957.

Degh, Linda. *Folktales of Hungary*. London: Routledge & Kegan Paul, 1965.

Downing, Charles. *Armenian Folktales and Fables*. Oxford: Oxford University Press, 1993.

Downing, Charles. *Russian Tales and Legends*. Oxford: Oxford University Press, 1996.

Fillmore, Parker. *Czech, Moravian, and Slovak Fairy Tales*. New York: Hippocrene Books, 1998.

Fillmore, Parker. *The Laughing Prince: Jugoslav Folk and Fairy Tales*. New York: Harcourt, Brace & Co., 1921.

Hudec, Ivan. *Tales From Slavic Myths*. Wauconda, Illinois: Bolchazy–Carducci Publishers, 2001.

Huggins, Edward. *Blue and Green Wonders and Other Latvian Tales*. New York: Simon & Schuster, 1971.

Jirasek, Alois. *Old Czech Legends*. London: Forest Books, 1992.

Kavcic, Vladimir. *The Golden Bird: Folktales From Slovenia*. Cleveland, Ohio: The World Publishing Co., 1969.

Kuniczak, W.S. *The Glass Mountain: 26 Ancient Polish Folktales and Fables*. New York: Hippocrene Books, 1992.

Maas, Selve. *The Moon Painters and Other Estonian Folktales*. New York: The Viking Press, 1971.

Oparenko, Christina. *Ukranian Folktales*. Oxford: Oxford University Press, 1996.

Pennington, Anne, and Peter Levi, trans. *Marko the Prince: Serbo–Croat Hero Songs*. London: Duckworth, 1984.

Petrovitch, Woislav. *Hero Tales and Legends of the Serbians*. London: George G. Harrap & Co., 1921. Another old one that is a great find.